SHOES

Written by Yvette Cragun ♥ Illustrated by Myra Romano

pink umbrella
books

ISBN: 978-1-949598-06-3 (Paperback)
ISBN: 978-1-949598-14-8 (Hardcover)

Published by Pink Umbrella Books (www.pinkumbrellapublishing.com)

Yvette Cragun, author
Shoes / Yvette Cragun

A young girl sneaks into her mom's closet and imagines the places she will go in the fabulous shoes she finds.

Library of Congress Control Number: 2019950795
Illustrations by Myra Romano
Illustrations © 2020 Myra Romano
Edited by Merry Gordon and Marnae Kelley

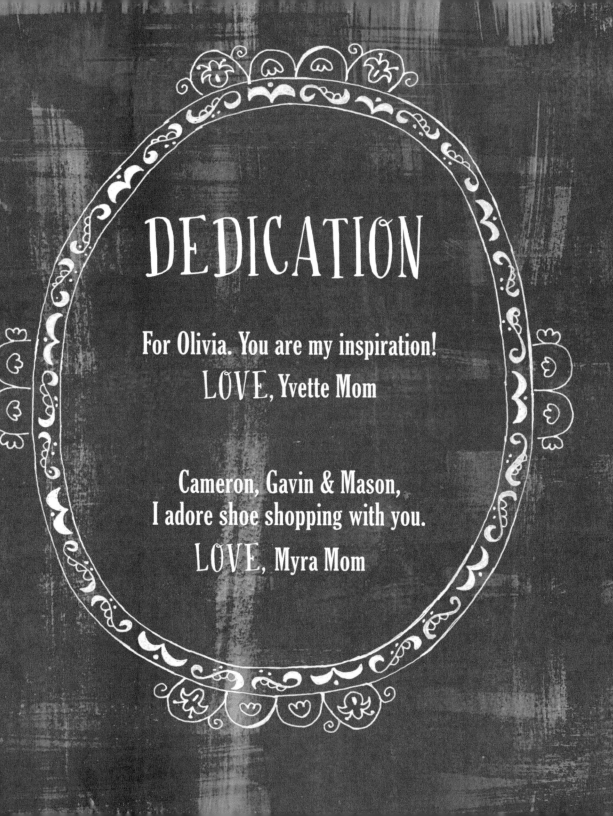

DEDICATION

For Olivia. You are my inspiration!
LOVE, Yvette Mom

Cameron, Gavin & Mason,
I adore shoe shopping with you.
LOVE, Myra Mom

Look at Mom's closet,
it's all full of shoes.

There are so many—
which ones shall I choose?

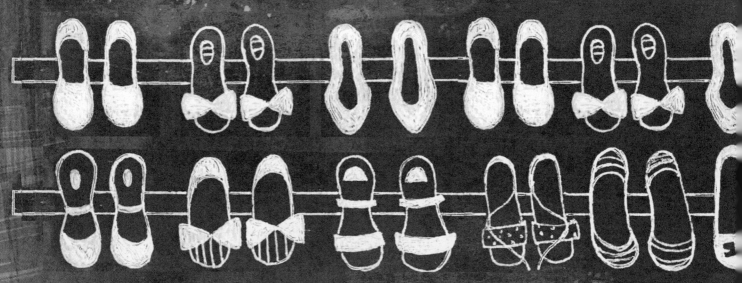

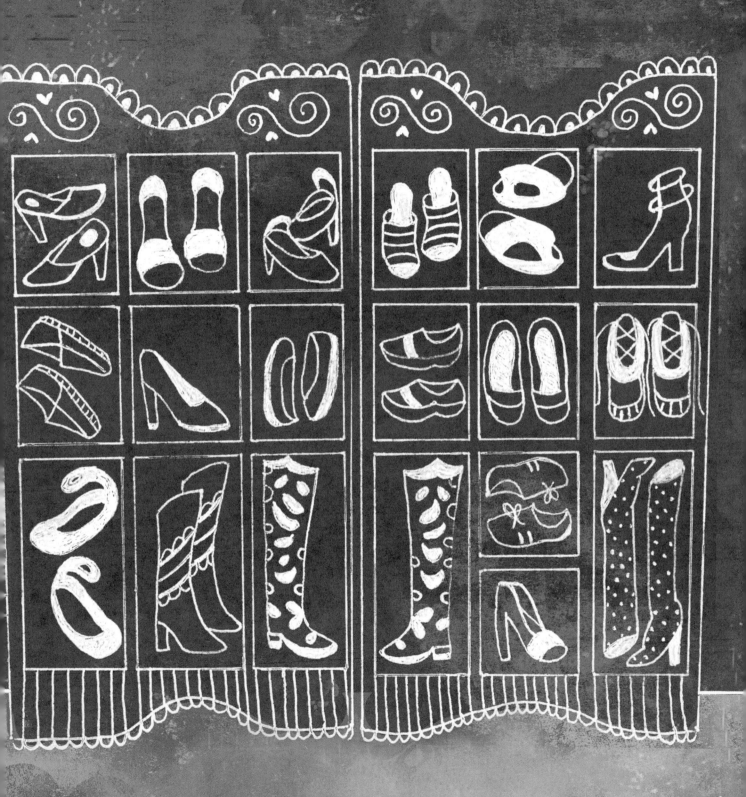

Shoes that have
buckles and satin and bows,

strappy and beaded
in perfect straight rows.

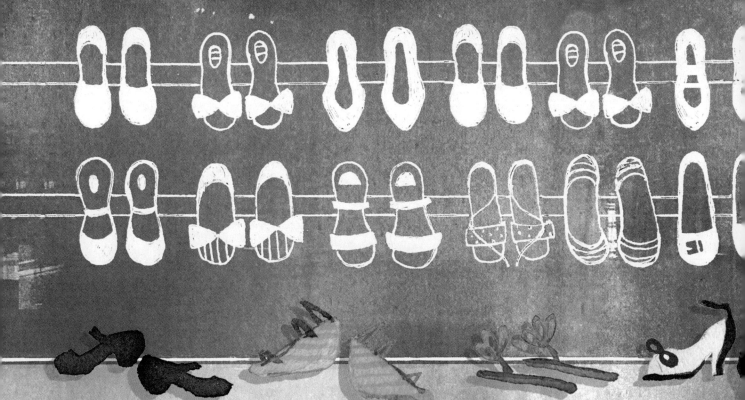

Pink ones for dancing
a graceful ballet.

Leaping and hopping,
I'd twirl through my day.

Cream ones are perfect
for parties with tea.

All of my friends will
have to agree.

Wedges are cute
and they're very in style.

I'll wear them to walk
on the beach for a while.

Flowery flip flops
are great by the pool.

Paired with a sundress,
I'll look super cool.

Red ones will sure
make my bright lipstick pop.

Rhinestones are lovely,
they sparkle on top.

Blue tennis shoes are
so cute and sporty.

Working out now,
I'll be fit when I'm forty.

Nothing can beat
a great pair of flats.

Comfy and sassy,
they're amazing with hats.

Black satin heels
are fancy and pretty.

Perfect for dining
at night in the city.

Who can decide just
which pair is best?

Mom won't miss one—
she can keep all the rest!

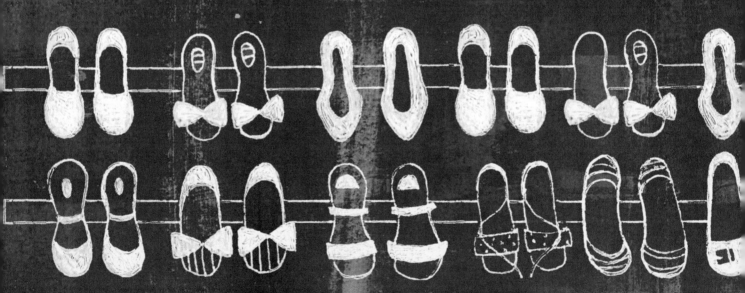

Mom calls me down to go play at the park.

"We need to go now before it gets dark!"

Sounds like such fun,
we will have a great time.

Best shoes for playing?
Definitely mine.

Made in the USA
Las Vegas, NV
27 August 2022